Rocket Dog

by Lynda Gore
Illustrated by Mark Penman

IGNITE

Titles in Ignite

Badger Publishing Limited
Suite G08, Stevenage,
Hertfordshire SG1 2DX
Telephone: 01438 791037   Fax: 01438 791036
www.badgerlearning.co.uk

Rocket Dog ISBN 978-1-84926-959-9

Text © Lynda Gore 2012
Complete work © Badger Publishing Limited 2012

Publisher: Susan Ross
Senior Editor: Danny Pearson
Designer: Fiona Grant
Illustrator: Mark Penman

Rocket Dog

Contents

Vocabulary:

inventor	babbled
reattach	disappointed
tinkering	churning

Main characters:

Craig

Grandad

Rocket Dog

Chapter 1

A project

Craig had asked his parents again for a dog but the answer was "NO!"

"I'm going out," he snarled and jumped on his bike to cycle to his Grandad's, just a few streets away.

Grandad, was an inventor, and spent most of his time in his shed.

"You will get a dog one day," said Grandad trying to cheer Craig up. "Come down to the shed," he continued, "I'm working on a project."

Craig shuddered. Not another project, he thought to himself. Some of Grandad's projects were a bit crazy.

But when Craig saw what Grandad had on his work bench he could not believe his eyes!

"I've been working on this for a while," Grandad babbled excitedly.

Craig looked at the machine, a long tubular body on four legs with wheels.

There was a long tail on one end and the other end had several wires hanging out.

"I'm building you a robot," explained Grandad. "But it needs a head."

"A robot dog!" beamed Craig. The grin on his face stretched from ear to ear.

"This is the best kind of dog," Grandad laughed. "You don't have to feed it, and no mess!"

Craig tried to think of something they could use for a head.

His little sister had a bag of old toys ready to give to a charity shop, perhaps he could look in there.

Craig quickly cycled home and returned to Grandad's with an old toy dog.

"Excellent," said Grandad. "Perfect!"

Craig and Grandad started to remove the head and reattach it to the robot dog. They worked for hours.

When they had finally finished, it was very late and dark.

"We will test him tomorrow," yawned Grandad.

Craig was a bit disappointed. He was eager to try out robot dog.

"Try and think of a good name for him," said Grandad.

They locked the shed door and walked back to the house.

Chapter 2

Out of control

Craig stayed at Grandad's house, but didn't sleep very well. He kept waking up.

First he thought he heard a funny noise.

Then a flash of light lit up his bedroom. Craig got up and looked out of the window.

He could see the light from the shed casting shadows across the grass.
He could hear the buzzing of the drill.

Grandad just couldn't stop tinkering, he thought.

Craig tiptoed down the stairs and opened the door to the garden.

He looked out. Everything was dark. Everything was quiet.

He must have been dreaming.

The next morning, Craig was up early.
He ran to the shed and opened the door.

The robot dog's eyes were glowing red.

Suddenly, it raced out of the shed.
It whizzed through Craig's legs and
darted around the garden.

It knocked over the rubbish bin.
It zoomed around Grandad's
vegetable patch, flattening most of the
plants.

Then it chased the neighbours' cat,
making it screech and spit.

Finally, it crashed through the fence
and disappeared down the street.

Craig was stunned.
"What just happened?" He whispered.

Grandad didn't know either. "I haven't connected the battery yet!" he spluttered. "He seemed to go like a rocket."

Craig thought this would be a perfect name, 'Rocket.'

"I will chase Rocket Dog," yelled Craig as he grabbed his bike.

Grandad was scratching his head.
"No need," he suddenly said. "Rocket is fitted with a dog-cam we can track him on-line."

Chapter 3

Big trouble

Craig and Grandad sat in front of the computer. They logged onto the dog-cam.

They could see an angry crowd and Rocket Dog seemed to be in the middle. There was trouble at the shopping mall.

"What has he done NOW?" gasped Craig.
And then the screen went black.

Craig jumped onto his bike and cycled
like crazy to the shopping mall.

Alarms and sirens were screaming.
Craig's stomach was churning.

He had a dreadful feeling that
something awful was about to happen.
There were so many people at the mall.
Craig couldn't see a thing.

He pushed through the crowd, he
needed to get to the front.
He needed to find out what had
happened to Rocket.

Craig's heart was thumping. Finally he reached the centre of the crowd.

A policeman picked up a mangled heap of metal from the road. "It was all over very quickly, son," said a voice from the crowd.

Craig looked at the junk in the policeman's hand. He saw a red eye flash once and then go out.

Craig instantly knew it was Rocket Dog. He was gone. Craig started to back away.

"WAIT!" boomed the policeman.

But Craig cycled back to his Grandad's as fast as he could.

Chapter 4

A visitor

It still wasn't clear what had happened at the shopping mall.

"It must have been a terrible accident," Craig told Grandad.

They decided to watch the dog-cam images.

"This looks like a raid," gasped Grandad.

As they watched, they saw a gang get into a fast car.

"Rocket was hit by the getaway car," sniffed Craig.

Suddenly, a loud knock at the front door made them both jump.

The policeman stood in the doorway with the mangled remains of Rocket Dog.

Craig just wanted to cry, he had only had the dog for a day.

Grandad showed the policeman the images from the dog-cam.

"That looks like Bugsy Marlow's gang," the policeman said. "We have been after him for years."

The policeman was very excited and told Grandad about the Crime Stoppers reward.

But Grandad refused it. "No amount of money would bring Rocket back," he said.

Craig looked at the heap of metal on the table. "He just needed a few tweaks," he whispered.

"We can try and rebuild him," Grandad suggested.

But Craig just wanted to go home. Rebuilding would take weeks.

The following week, Craig cycled past Grandad's house every day on his way to school.

He had seen the police van outside several times.

On Friday afternoon, he saw Grandad on the doorstep talking to a policeman. What was going on?

Craig hid his bike in the bushes.
He crept round behind the van and
listened.

"Well, we have visited you a few times
this week," the policeman said to
Grandad.

"I think everything will work out perfectly."

"Yes," agreed Grandad. "I know Craig will be very pleased with him."

Craig had to put his hand over his mouth, he was so excited. This could mean only one thing. They had fixed Rocket!

Chapter 5

Another project

After dinner on Friday evening, Craig went back to Grandad's.

"Come into the garden," said Grandad. "I've been working on another project."

Craig wasn't interested in another project. He wanted to see Rocket – the rebuild, the most amazing robot.

But as Craig raced into the garden, something caught his eye.

He saw a large, black shape. It travelled across the garden, running towards him.

A huge, black beast with teeth and mad eyes.

It knocked Craig down and then stood over him. Craig shut his eyes tight.

He could feel the hot breath on his face. This was certain death.

Then the beast started to... lick his face.

"His name is Jet," laughed Grandad. "He is a retired police dog."

"But where's Rocket?" asked Craig. "I heard you talking about him."

"No," said Grandad. "You heard me talking about Jet."

First Grandad had been to see Jet at
the re-homing centre. Then a police-dog
handler visited Grandad.

"We are responsible for looking after
Jet now," added Grandad.

Craig looked at Jet. He was so cool.
They chased around the garden together.

Craig hid things and Jet found them.
He threw a ball and Jet caught it.
Until, finally, they both fell into a heap
on the grass.

Craig felt he had known Jet forever.

"We can look after him together," Grandad smiled and put his arm around Craig's shoulder.

Craig had to admit this was Grandad's best project ever.

Police dogs

Police dogs are especially chosen for their courage, agility and strength.

Some breeds are more suitable for the role of a police dog than others.

The most popular breeds used are German Shepherd, Springer Spaniel and Cocker Spaniel.

Police dogs are usually retired when they reach eight or nine years old, or younger if they become injured or ill.

Crime Stoppers

Crime Stoppers is a charity helping to find criminals and help solve crimes.

The charity operates a free phone number and web site for members of the public to report crime anonymously.

Crime Stoppers pay anything from £50 to £1000 reward for information that leads to an arrest and conviction.

5 Dog jokes

Q. What do you get if you cross a sheepdog with a rose?
A. A collie-flower

Q. How do you find your dog if he is lost in the woods?
A. Put your ear up to a tree and listen for the bark

Q. What do you get if you cross a dog with a lion?
A. A terrified postman

Q. What kind of dog wears contact lenses?
A. A Cock-eyed Spaniel

Q. Which dog can tell the time?
A. A watchdog

Questions

Where did Craig find a head for the robot dog?

What did the robot dog chase around the garden?

What was the name of robot dog?

What did the robot dog record on its dog-cam?

What was the huge, black beast with teeth and mad eyes at the end of the story?